for Arielle & Kaya

The Sly Fox of the Mind

Written by Brooke Olstein & Lee Scharfstein

Illustrated by Geraldina Sierra

One day a little girl named Shanty came home from school and said to her Mommy, "Mommy, Jennifer said that I am not pretty."

The Mommy thought for a second and then asked her little daughter, "Who gets to say that you are pretty?"

With tears rolling down her face she pointed at her Mom.

Her mom shook her head "No" and pointed back at her, "No... you are the one that gets to say that you are pretty."

Little Shanty crawled up into her Mom's arms and said "But Mommy, it makes me so upset."

The mom smiled at Shanty and said; "Let me tell you a story about the Sly Fox and the Good Fox."

"The Sly fox lives in your head and tells you things that aren't true. So the sooner you can learn to recognize when it's the Sly Fox who's talking, the sooner you'll be able take your power back from him, and fill your head with all the good stuff that is true."

Shanty looked at her Mom eagerly, "So how do I know it's the Sly Fox?"

"It is very easy", Shanty's Mom replied.
"Here are the signs and the feelings
you have when it's the Sly Fox"...

You feel mad... You feel bad...

You feel angry... You feel confused...

You feel sad... You feel jealous...

You feel ungrateful... You feel sorry for yourself...

You feel embarrassed and all you care about is what others think of you...

Shanty asked her mom "What are some of the things that the Sly Fox might say to me?"

"The Sly Fox will tell you things like... You are not good enough...

You are not smart... You are not loved...

Why does he or she get all the attention and not me?... You are not doing it right... You shouldn't try because you might get embarrassed or look stupid...

You're not as pretty or handsome as another... You don't deserve it."

The Mom said to her daughter, "There are many things and sometimes the Sly Fox might be in the head of your friend or a classmate. It is your job to be aware; and just as quickly, you can claim your power back from the lies that are only attempting to take your light away."

Shanty looked at her Mom, "But how do I do that?"

"Well, noticing it is the first step. And then calling the Sly Fox out will allow you to take the last step, which is completely destroying the thoughts that the Sly Fox has told you."

Shanty smiled and nodded at her Mom hesitantly.

Shanty's Mom said, "Okay, try this. Reach up and grab that imaginary sly fox out of your head and throw it out the window...

Or, if you prefer, imagine putting those bad thoughts in a balloon of the color of your choice, and let it fly far far away. And when it reaches a safe distance, clap your hands and pop it and the thoughts will disappear in to the air."

"Will the Sly Fox ever come back?" asked Shanty.

"Oh, he will be back," said Shanty's Mom. "The Sly Fox is there to test you and it is up to you to master dealing with the Sly Fox.

See, what you're really doing is learning to love the parts of you that say those things, and then replacing them with The Good Fox."

"I knew there had to be a Good Fox," said Shanty excitedly.

Shanty's Mom smiled wide, "The Good Fox will advise you to look in the mirror and say things like... I am perfect just the way I am...

I am smart in my own way... I am beautiful inside and out... I am loved, loving and loveable...

I love myself the way I am... I am the LIGHT... I am powerful and strong...

I am responsible for what I say and do... I am a magnet for Good."

Shanty had a big smile too now. But then she began to look a little worried. "But what if I forget?" Shanty asked.

Her mom lovingly said, "Then I will remind you."

"You can teach everyone and be a light in the world. You are here to shine your light and love your shadow. The Good Fox also wants you to know something very important.

When you hear things at school or even sometimes from your own parents, just remember two things... 'Don't take it personally' and always do your best."

Shanty was smiling at the relief of releasing the Sly Fox and not being pretty enough...

The next day they were driving in the car and the radio came on playing their favorite song and Shanty called her mom from the back, "Mom, sometimes I don't get rid of the Sly Fox. I dance with it."

Shanty's mom smiled and said, "That's my girl!"

THE END

Made in the USA
Middletown, DE
09 June 2016